Second Edition

Secrets of the Southern Shells

Timeless Wisdom for Southern Shells and Other Belles

by Casey Tennyson with photography and art by the author
and illustrations by Katelyn Tennyson Swann

In 2010, my 18-year-old daughter read the manuscript and quipped, "This is what you tell me everyday. The starfish is giving me a lecture." *Perfect.* The book then achieved it's mission to capture the intimate communication inside the homes of Southern Shells. ~ Author Casey Tennyson

Praise

"*Secrets of the Southern Shells* is a very clever and original allegory containing much wisdom that has been passed down from Southern mothers to their daughters, the Southern Belles. This charming book, filled with very attractive marine artwork, relates a powerful story of sea creatures, and how one, a mere starfish, overcomes impossible obstacles and achieves her dreams because she faithfully heeds her mother's timeless advice. In seven words: Buy it, read it, and gift it!" — Bill Guggenheim, co-author of bestseller *Hello From Heaven!* "p.s. I read this while vacationing in North Carolina. It's not a book I would typically read. I was surprised at how much I liked it. The book cleverly combined three or four things in one masterfully."

"This is a book to cherish and re-read often as we follow the life challenges of Starfish Star and relate them to our own lives and to the lives of our children and grandchildren. This book is destined to be a classic."
-Marilyn Smith, Mental Health Therapist

"I'm from South Georgia and have two daughters and this is the way we talk to them. I look at the whole world this way; speak from the heart and from personal experience. The world is a better place if we all share our hearts. I liked the chapter with the seahorses on how small things make a big difference, it's important for all of us to remember that each little act every day does make a difference."
~ Hugh Darley, President / Executive Producer Idea, Inc.

"I got this as a retirement gift and it is special on so many levels. The illustrations, the sentiments and especially a mother – daughters love resonated so strongly having raised two daughters myself. A perfect gift to yourself or someone who has impacted your life in a meaningful way." –Barbara Peckett, Director of New Business Development, Clear Channel Orlando

"I got the book as a hostess gift and what a lovely surprise. The book creatively captures the author's love of shells, the beach and the water. If you love Florida and it's waters, you will love the book. I move the book around the house, it speaks to many occasions." — Ernestine Beattie, Olympic Swimmer and Champion Master Swimmer (fellow water lover!)

Title:
Secrets of the Southern Shells
Second Edition

Published by:
Cutting Edge Communications, Inc.

Written by:
Casey Tennyson
with art and photography by the author

Illustrations by:
Katelyn Tennyson Swann

International Standard Book Number
ISBN number 978-0-9855264-2-9

Dedication

DEDICATION

This book is dedicated with love to my daughter Katelyn on her 18th birthday, and to my son Carter. This book reflects the Southern Spirit within us. Our heritage flows through us from parents to children, and to future generations to come.

The first edition I wrote in 2010 as Katelyn left for college. The second edition in 2015 coincides with her college graduation and her new adventures into adulthood. She contributed her artistic ability for illustrations in this edition, such as the first sketch of "Ollie" above. As a student, she took art classes in school, local art schools and studios, and private lessons. Her art garnered kudos as it was often chosen for the student exhibit at the internationally acclaimed Winter Park Sidewalk Art Festival and Maitland Art Festival. She continued art studies at New College of Florida where she got a psychology degree. She is a prolific artist and talented animator.

In her childhood, Katelyn was either playing with her pets or drawing them. Her destiny to be a vet or an artist was apparrent at a young age.

I don't have a southern accent or the life experiences of my mother or her prominent Southern family. I grew up in Florida with Tara-esque images from family summer vacations to antebellum homes filled with genteel voices in Tennessee and Mississippi.

My children and I are descendants of British and Scottish colonists on both my mother and father's side. On my mother's side, the Doak family founded the first college in what would become the state of Tennessee. Her family members founded the first Presbyterian churches, also. They were among the first political leaders in Charlotte and the state of North Carolina. A few generations later, my grandfather continued the legacy as a State Representative for Tennessee a few terms and mayor of his small town. They all contributed much to the essence of freedom and liberty that would become The United States of America. As each generation travels further from our Southern base and culture, and as my own children enter adulthood, I felt a desire to capture some of the Southern words of wisdom I would hope they would share with their own children one day.

In the Bahamas spring 2010, the book was conceptualized, *Secrets of the Southern Shells*, drawing from my southern heritage and also my intense respect and love of the ocean.

My journal could be *Memories of a Mermaid* as I was splashing, floating or boating in the water many of my waking hours. Summer 2010, I spent beach time in Florida at New Smyrna Beach, Palm Beach, The Keys, with quick trips to Clearwater and Naples, as well as trips to the islands. Throughout my life, I have visited nearly every beach in Florida deciding which one to call home as my children go to college.

My favorite people have played in the water with me. I played with childhood friends in lakes ... swim team friends (I was captain) ... synchronized swimming friends with matching swim suits ... University of Central Florida surf team buddies in contests (I was one of the first three girls on the UCF surf team) ... my children and Winter Park's Park Grove neighbor toddlers in my back yard pool learning to swim ... many, many family and friends beach trips all over Florida and much of the world ... boating with friends in the U.S. from Kennebunkport to the Florida Keys ... I am happiest on anything that floats from surf-boards, to kayaks to boats of any size.

Contents

20 Tips for Southern Shells and Other Belles
While the global world has changed extensively over the last 200 years since the birth of America and the Southern U.S., the intimate advice from Southern mothers to their children has remained virtually unchanged. Sometimes as adults we need a little reminder, also.

Remember who you are,
you are a Southern Star.

CONTENTS

Dedication
Author's Preface

CHAPTERS

Be Careful
What You
Wish For

BE CAREFUL WHAT YOU WISH FOR

Starfish Star floated over the coral. She gazed through the reflective ripples up high into the twilight spring sky and searched for the first hint of a celestial sparkle.

"Star light, star bright, first star I see to-night, I wish I may, I wish I might, have the wish I wish tonight," she whispered just to herself.

She closed her eyes tightly with all her might feeling her long eyelashes tickling her face, and every tiny suction cup on her tips clenched with fervor as she presented her wishes to the heavens. In her childhood her wishes were bountiful and her visions expansive for a Southern Shell. She believed she could have anything she wanted in the whole world. *Her mother told her to be careful what she wished for because surely her wish would come true because she was a Southern Shell.* She was loved dearly.

She delighted in a quiet recollection of all the many wishes already come true and those wishes yet to be dreamed. Star loved to star gaze and twilight was certainly her favorite time of each day.

Remember Who You Are
You Are A
Southern Star

REMEMBER WHO YOU ARE,
YOU ARE A SOUTHERN STAR

Star's mother's wishes for Star were quite different from Star's own. Her mother wished Star would be content and happy in their seaside home. She was loved and safe tucked next to the rocky inlet, across from the red lighthouse, beside the white sugar sand dunes. For over 200 years, the Star family had played and thrived, lived and died in the turquoise water of the Southern Shores.

The Star family had originally come from across the ocean on a grand sailing vessel to start the new Star Colony. Star had always been proud of her heritage of spiritual, strong leaders with handsome moral men and beautiful sweet women. To perpetuate the heritage, Star felt an urging to accomplish her own dreams of creating goodness in the world beyond the safety of Star Colony and the Southern Shores. Star's mother acknowledged her daughter's adventurous spirit, boundless aspirations and expansive vision. *She encouraged Star to remember who you are on the journey.* Star's mother knew Star would venture out into the world to fulfill her destiny.

Be Sweet

BE SWEET

Shell, Star's best childhood friend had a soft, creamy white coating with a smooth sheen and the most delicate five-point flower design on her back. Star had more of a tan textured coating and felt quite tall next to her dearest friend. The two were inseparable and inextricably linked on the Southern Shores. Shell's family had also been among the original shells of the Colony, and the two were quite the same under their differing sizes, shapes and colors. What bound them the most was the sweetness in their souls, a gift inherited from each of their mothers. *Be sweet they were told daily.* The friendship would be eternal, as to be sweet to one another would surely bind them for life as it had generations of the mothers themselves.

While Shell epitomized seaside beauty and demure persona, sweetness itself, Star commanded much of the attention along the shore. Among the other Stars, she stood out with her slightly taller body and her perky prance. Her trails across the sand would gleefully be followed by the other shells looking for fun and adventure. Star thrived in the vast attention and delighted in her uniqueness in the sea of sameness.

Let Boys Find You

LET BOYS FIND YOU

  Star's favorite activity was joining Clam and the other shells for body surfing each day on the other side of the tide pool in the gentle rolling white froth washing up to the Star Colony border. She would wait for him to come by each day to invite her to play, as girls were not to seek boys in Star Colony. *Don't call boys she had been told. Let boys find you.* The childhood training was designed so Star could attract the proper mate when the time was right. Boy shells in the Star Colony had been taught the same proper manners and etiquette. She did want a fine man Star and a beach full of little Starlets one day.

  Up and down, twist and twirl, Star delighted in the thrill of actually being a part of the wave. Clam used his strong muscles to propel himself by clapping and clamping his shells shut. Star kept up with him by paddling her five arms, and the duo played for hours in the shimmer of the morning surf.

Combine

COMBINE SOUTHERN HOSPITALITY WITH COMPASSION

Back on the beach, gregarious Star made friends daily. She often picnicked with the beach guests and posed for photos. She got a ride in a white wicker basket with a yellow daisy design on a shiny red beach bike. With the whoosh, whoosh of the pedals, the balmy salt air current kissing her face made her feel she could fly like a shooting star right out of the basket. Star so wanted to fly high in the air like the stars of the heavens she admired and wished upon each evening.

From the basket, she got to travel to the whole dog beach on the other side of the inlet. A drenched dripping French Bulldog from the dog beach followed the bike over to Star Colony. Star invited him to an afternoon game of hide-and-seek with her and the crabs. The dog had a hard time hiding because of his enormous size. He barked at the holes giving away the crabs hiding places and barked at the bright yellow plastic bucket where Star had impishly hidden. Dogs she decided might be better friends for other games. *Have different friends for different dimensions of your life, her mother had told her. Have many friends and they will all have a special part of your life and make you a better person. Your Southern Hospitality will draw people to you and a genuine compassion and caring will keep them near, she had learned.*

Star's favorite hiding place was inside of sand castles constructed on the shore daily. Each day there would be a new gleaming castle estate to explore. She would pretend she was a real princess in a faraway land. Star wanted to travel the world and see a sunrise and sunset from every coast on every continent. Goals are good.

Help Your Neighbors

HELP YOUR NEIGHBORS

This morning was special in the Star Colony. The loggerheads had hatched. Friends of both sand and sea, the mama Loggerheads were the most respected of the elders, some 300 years old, older than the Star Colony itself. The whole shore waited patiently for the turtle egg nest to hatch baby turtles bound for the deep sea. Star ran past the scattering of crumbled eggshells dotting the shore, to cheer them on in their first few tentative steps toward the sea. Their arms and legs would build strength pushing on the grainy soft sand to prepare them for entering the surf and learning to swim. The waves were particularly choppy and treacherously high this day and Star was concerned for her tiny round newborn friends.

A surfer girl noticed the plight of the baby turtles tossing in the shore break under hungry circling seagulls. She gathered two and put them on the tip of her stealth red surfboard. Star got caught up in the excitement and thrill of adventure, and hopped up on the board, too. *Be neighborly and offer help when needed, her mother advised often.* The trio bobbed and splashed and squealed with excitement as the crest of the waves splashed over the smooth fiberglass plane. Star, even with all of her suction cups pressed against the surf wax, had difficulty holding her stance. The newborns, still sticky from their eggs, slid left to right to be gently tucked back to safety each time by the surfer girl.

Star watched the clear water under the board turn aqua, turquoise and then to a rich royal blue as the inches turned to fathoms. After some time of up and down and to and fro, the team was past the shore break and the baby turtles bravely hopped into the sea. Star jumped off, too, but could not dive as deeply as the turtles. She was accustomed to the tide pool where she could touch the bottom, and this by contrast was quite deep and a bit spooky.

Photo: turtle tracks at left. Please don't litter on the beach. The turtles mistake plastic for jellyfish. They eat the plastic, which causes health issues or death.

Take Time For Yourself

Never miss a chance to travel, or shop, or spa. Life is short, so enjoy yourself. Reward yourself for accomplishments, her mother would encourage her. Experiencing the deep water for the first time, Star breathed in a big salty deep breath and floated for a moment letting the ebb and flow massage her tired arms. She was so excited to be here. So deep! Star kicked in glee against the rich blue sheath splashing white cylinders high in the air and tumbling down in a cascade of circles floating away fading to blue again. "Splish splash I'm free. Splish splash see me," she sang as she experienced her buoyant independence. But who was to notice her in this independent moment? Who was to hear her song? Star glanced around and realized the turtles now had disappeared deep below the cobalt blue. In the shallow shore, you could see to the bottom. Here you could not.

Travel, shop, spa!

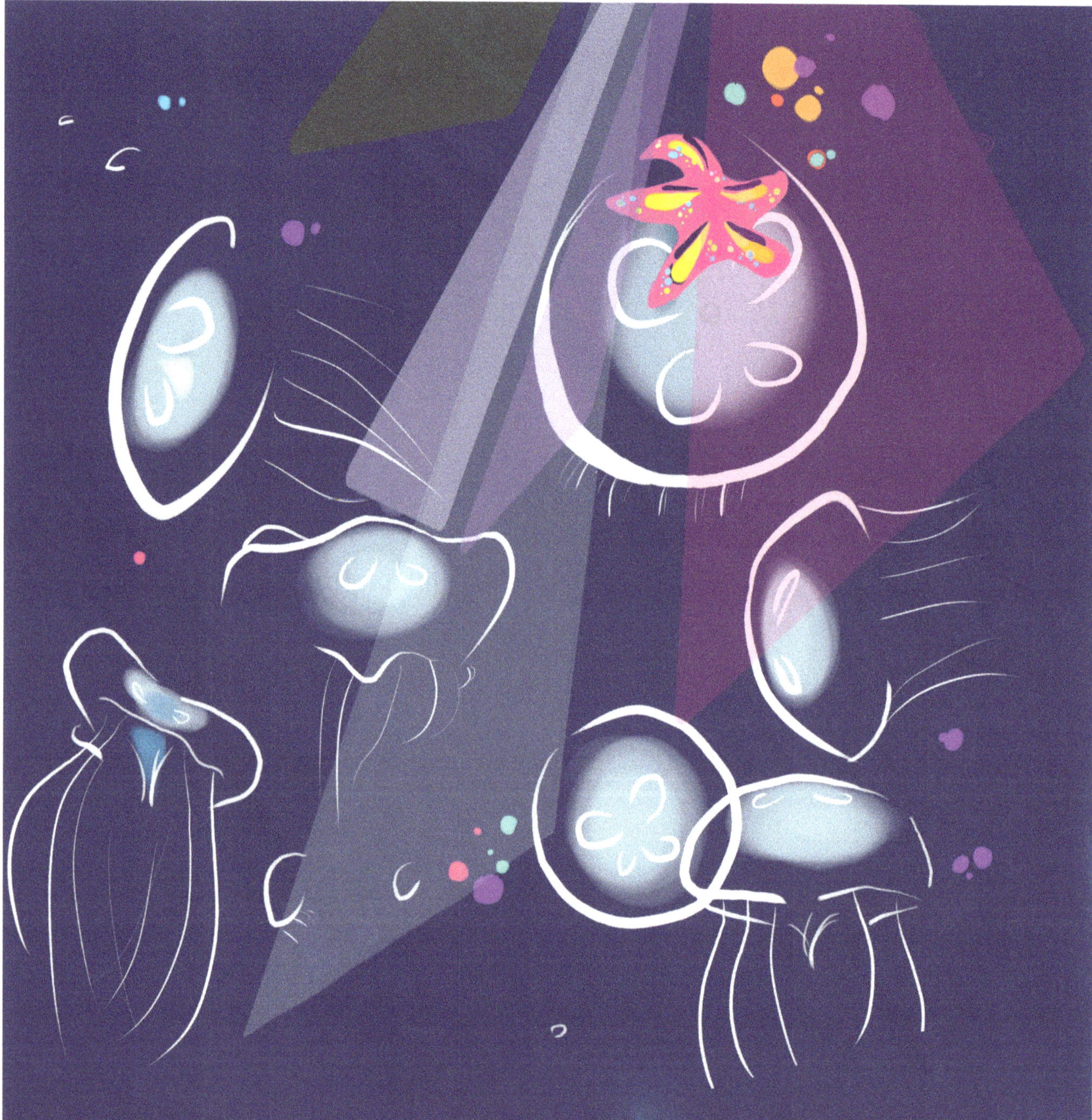

Kill Meanness With
Kindness

KILL MEANNESS WITH KINDNESS

 A group of iridescent slippery sirens noticed Star's alarm. Their nature was to be hurtful rather than helpful. They beckoned and called and teased and taunted Star that she couldn't swim further. In their race past her, one flung a tentacle against her arm and stung her ever so slightly. A more direct sting would have been quite severe. *In the flurry of the flow of the moment, Star could hear her mother's words. When you feel the sting of meanness then kill with kindness.* She would like to have shown her Southern Charm, however, she chose to be strong and silent and simply smile, on the outside anyway. It hurt. Being quiet at times can show greater kindness than words she had learned. The ones who sting often feel the sting of their own poison the most. Star had been told it was best simply to feel sorry for those who sting.

Stay In Safe Places
With Safe People

STAY IN SAFE PLACES WITH SAFE PEOPLE

The thrill seeking now had a sting of reality not only with her throbbing arm, but now with an acknowledgement that she would not make it back to Star Colony before nightfall. Fear of the unfamiliar in the flow of an unknown world swept through her mind as a rip tide was now sweeping her from the royal delft blue to the navy blue water. *Her mother had warned her, don't swim alone and stay where I can see you. Stay in safe places with safe people.*

The overprotective mothering oracle now would be a welcomed sound to the exasperated and exhausted Star. The splish and splash now in solitary stillness felt more like a tick and a tock against her still body. "Tick tock tick tock the clock of doom," she feared.

Hold
Your
Head
High

HOLD YOUR HEAD HIGH

In the deep, danger was not a warning but a rapid-fire reality of live and die. Star was now not of the shore, but of the endless deep, where large fish feed on smaller ones. A ten-foot silver and blue marlin cracked open the seal of the sea surface and with bill thrust high, soared aloft in the air past Star in a show of power and valor. He greyhounded onward with incredible speed toward the setting sun in the horizon. *Stunned, she instinctively held her head high. That is what her mother would have told her to do. Don't show fear or vulnerability. Be confident in every situation.* You are a Southern Shell. Adversaries prefer the weak over the able. This massive pelagic predator was showing off to his confident admirer more than seeking conflict with her she realized. She was a bit uneasy after the brush with the jellyfish but quickly shifted to admiration for this giant protector of the sea.

Be Independent

BE INDEPENDENT

  The ocean was alive with action as a sea plane flew over head,
a fishing yacht motored by, and a group of sailboats floated in
the distance. Surely the children who played with her during
the days on the shore would see her and stop by to pick her up
as they always did and take her back to Star Colony to safety.
She waved and waved and yet went unnoticed as the whirrs of
the engines faded from deafening to barely audible. Out of her
element and environment, far away from Star Colony, she was
just another ripple of life in an expansive floating fluid.
  On the horizon, the white sport fishing yacht with the spar-
kling silver tuna tower now had the iridescent marlin caught
on a fishing line fully lit, flying high and fighting for life in
a tug of wills. The thrashing and splashing of the mammoth
fish from afar gave a spectacular show of the beauty of nature
silhouetted against the azure firmament.
  While the marlin had shown great strength and pride, his
ability to protect Star with his sharp bill and masculine phy-
sique changed dramatically as the fisherman's hook sank into
the flesh of his mouth. *Star could hear her mother's words telling
her to be polite and graciously accept assistance and encouragement
from others, but ultimately be independent and rely upon yourself.*

Always Look For
Something Good

ALWAYS LOOK FOR
SOMETHING GOOD

The sinking tangerine sun over the orange painted bands and the drama of the sailfish saga gave way to an even darker and scarier twilight. Star was all alone in the world. She cried out but only heard the pulsating of her own small voice along the glassy void. In the open sea, without the safety of the inlet at Star Colony, the crests tossed her slightly airborne to rest again on the surface until the next rhythmic bounce. In this pro-cess of to and fro, she felt neither a part of the sea or the air, and not the land, which she had left some time ago. She was in a trinity un-reality, not altogether belonging anywhere, and deeply longing with all of her heart for home at the Southern Shores.

Twinkle, twinkle called the first star of the night sky and beckoned Star for her wish of the day. Star without hesitation responded, "fam-ily." She concentrated on the good. Star didn't have the Star family, but still had the familiarity and comfort of the stars of the sky. *Star's mother always said, you can find good in every situation you just have to look. There must be good here somewhere.*

Replace Fear
With Faith

REPLACE FEAR WITH FAITH

As she closed her eyes, she saw the colors of the day. The vibrant hues of blue fading now into impending darkness. The full moon added a hint of white light to the rippling cobalt blanket that now became her comfort for the evening. In total exhaustion and exasperation, Star made a convex bowl shape like the turtles she followed out only this morning. She rolled on her back and with her tiny waterlogged tips pointing toward the rising stars, she attempted to put the day to rest.

Restlessness replaced rest in waves of fear. The fear was manageable she found as shadows, sounds and illusions faded by replacing the fear with hope and faith. She found the fear of fearfulness to be the most debilitating in her waffling in the waves. This afternoon, in fear she moved and progressed, but here in anticipation of fear, she sat in stillness in the salty emptiness. *Replace fear with faith rang in her head from her childhood teachings.*

Use Words Wisely

USE WORDS WISELY

The turbulence within her distracted her from the severity of the mountains of water. The salt of her own tiny tears flavored her face along with the baked sea salt flaking and pressing against her cheeks. Star rarely cried. If you truly believed good always comes from bad, then bad does not exist for long, then you should not shed tears, right? These tears gave no choice as the streaming release of the day flowed from out of herself. Her cry was curt. She was surprised to have cried at all.

The analytical aftermath provided some mental stimulation in the solitude. Star floated, sighed, cried but mostly just breathed in and out from one tip to the next. The buoyancy of her breath she realized was life itself. She became acutely aware of the sound of her own faint breath against the crashing waves.

Even with all the attention given to her in Star Colony, her voice was fainted against the backdrop of the rolling tide and the activities of the other shells.

Far from the shore, her voice bounced off the walls of water, vibrating into grand sounds she had never heard before. She had never really listened to her own voice. Here in the quiet, she couldn't not hear and what spoke loudly was, "I am alone."

Use words wisely as they have great power. Her mother's words now were present with her own. She listened this time to the remembrance of her mother's words and carefully chose the next words she would shout to the wall of water. She redirected her thoughts from fear to fantasy. "I am alone. I am alone with the man I am to marry," she added the happy ending to the sentence and to her reality. That put a smile on her face and made her relax into the wish to know true love that she spoke to the heavens on many twilights.

She felt the water around her sparkle into a sea of sapphires with diamond tips. Her new perspective pleased her.

Listen to Your
Voice Inside

LISTEN TO YOUR VOICE INSIDE

Not her own voice or her mother's
voice this time, but Star heard that
little voice inside giving comfort
knowing safety was sure to come.
Look. *Listen to your voice inside.* Safety
came in a big round ball. A bobbing
red buoy appeared in the current and
Star climbed up for night's rest.

Do
Good
Work

DO GOOD WORK

Star spotted one lone frigate bird in a quiet contemplative flight back to shore. He was alone like her, yet the frigate was dancing in the breeze against the dark sky. He was singing to himself to celebrate a successful day of fishing, not only for himself but for the other birds, and also for fishermen he led to the schools of fish. While his work was to scout, he added to the good of the whole with his diligence and fortitude. Star decided her adventure would help the Star Colony. Just like the bird, Star would do good work and share her abundance. *She had been taught that you share your gifts and do good work.* Be a light unto others. She would add to the body of knowledge of life in the deep and share when she returned to shore.

Small
Counts
Big

SMALL COUNTS BIG

Star woke to the whirring motor of a sport fishing yacht coming right towards the buoy. Under her safe haven, she saw the active diminutive bait fish hiding from the circling wahoo and dolphin in the tangled trawlers net below. Whirrrr ... the boat came closer with the outriggers spread to the sides pulling behind colorful vibrant lures dancing on long clear lines. In a flurry of action, everyone was chasing everyone else. From her perch atop the safety of the buoy, she took note that the smallest of the fishes determined where everyone else would spend their morning. *Small has power of it's own she remembered. Without the small, there is no big.* She perked up at this thought but reminded herself she was quite far from home still. She took advantage of the chaos created from the dual waves from the wake of the boat and swan dived into the turquoise center of the current pointing towards shore.

Yes, shore! A dot of a red lighthouse blinked into sight. She saw a glimpse of a tiny ribbon of white sand beach with an icing layer of tiny emerald bead like shapes. The sea was glassy and the current was effortlessly gliding her directly toward the land so she relaxed and enjoyed the ride.

A morning parade of bouncing sea horses galloped by Star. A few clung to her tips and helped to pull her along as they cheerily swam for shore. She enjoyed their added propulsion and their positive energy. Yes, small has positive power! Small makes a difference, indeed.

Seek Wisdom

SEEK WISDOM

Star followed the current to shore but it was not her lighthouse and not her inlet. It didn't appear to be anybody's shore at all. The beach was eroded and the inlet weathered with time. Where were the shells on this deserted island of brokenness and solitude? In the lapping of loneliness she only found pieces of faded sharp broken shells and piles of itchy dried sea weed. At least the deep nurtured turtles and jellyfish and bait fish and marlins ... she questioned, was little voice inside wrong?

Seek wisdom her mother would have told her. Who here would know where to go?

A happy baritone hummed tune broke her momentary insecurity. The island fisherman with the oversized straw hat responded to her predicament and to her effervescent Southern Spirit for which she had been well trained. He scooped her up into his rowboat of wood with peeling paint in a bucket tucked beside cane poles and fishing line. He sang a song with a cheerful beat and promised little Star he would help take her to the inlet with a bounty of Stars. She was relieved to have found someone who knew the island and who could get her to her inlet. She was overflowing with gratitude.

And the fisherman inquired ... Did not your family leave their land? Did not they choose to seek liberty and freedom? So, be as you must be and do as you must do. And when lost, you will not lose your way. Trust your heart. It is your shore you rely upon, but really it's your God among the stars. You see His tides from every shore and His stars from every sky. The fisherman's voice was a song of peaceful notes between the splashes of the wooden oars.

Wait For
The Right One

WAIT FOR THE RIGHT ONE

The inlet popped into sight. The wise fisherman was right, Star families with little stars filled the beach. Sand dollars and shells of every size and shape danced and sparkled in the crystal pink sand. The Stars were a little larger than Stars of Star Colony, and a little more brown from the tropical sun. This was a Star Colony for certain, but not her Star Colony. Fatigue and travel weariness dissipated as Star's social nature perked her up. She was so very happy to see Stars. She was also quite relieved to know that her little voice inside was right because she called upon it often.

Star hopped off the boat onto the beach. She noticed a dozen sand castles and sea glass and driftwood placed in the sand in X's and O's and the word "love" greeting her.

Star's mother's voice whispered, wait for the right one. You will know when it happens. He will find you.

Star heard a song from a young gentleman Star singing, "Here on the shore wait no more ... here you are, my little Southern Star."

Star light, star bright and all those wishes on all those stars of the sky and now here he was right before her.

Under the full vibrant reflective moon that evening, she tucked herself in a sea of clear. For everything was clear. She knew that she could have anything she wanted in the whole world because she was a Southern Shell. It wasn't what her mother had wanted for her, or anything she could have possibly dreamed from the Star Colony, but it was exactly what her heart truly desired.

She was patient and waited, was quiet and still, ventured out and ventured back, partied and played, held and stayed, and she got her wish, her every dream, her forever-after. She found her way and in the in-between found her family that was to be.

... exactly what
her heart
truly desired.

Be A Lady

Southern Shells
are not taught to simply ACT like a lady
but to actually BE a lady.

BE A LADY

To Be a Lady is the true secret of a Southern Shell, in every situation, for every challenge and celebration alike.

Far, far from the Star Colony, Star's understanding of the Southern Shell Secrets, encouraged her to help others, saved her from severe stings and sharp stabs, helped her understand and honor others, allowed her to show courage and express gratitude, kept her safe and loved, and ultimately delivered her to her heart's desire and destiny.

Being true unto herself, Star actually did please her mother. Southern Shells are not taught to simply act like a lady but to actually be a lady. The being implies living. Be who you are meant to be. Be with whom you are deeply drawn. Be and live where you shall. To be a lady is in your inner being and you take it inside you to any shore. To be a lady does not require perfection, but within the inevitable imperfection, be sweet and beautiful.

In the cadence of a contemporary world, as tides shift and winds weather the Southern Shores, Southern Shells know their secret is not a place or a person but in being, and living their heritage and culture within their hearts.

* 9 7 8 0 9 8 5 5 2 6 4 2 9 *